Kingdom of Horrors:

Bowels of Madness

A **DIMLIGHT** novella by

MARIOS KOUTSOUKOS

Copyright © 2018 Marios Koutsoukos

All rights reserved.

ISBN: 9798593562081

Cover artwork by Manthos Stergiou / Manster
Design: www.mansterdesign.com

Dimlight official site: www.dimlightband.com

"And of madness there are two kinds; one produced by human infirmity, the other a divine release of the soul from the yoke of custom and convention".

(Plato, *Phaedrus*, 265)

I

BIRTH OF AN EMPIRE

No great and beautiful thing lasts for long under the sun of this world. Man's happiness, however well-founded and certain it may seem, soon withers away. And so, too, do his empires. Even the mightiest ones.

Thus, it should come as no surprise to the student of that chain of human tragedies called history that the powerful empire of the Adamites was reduced to ruins in a span of a few short years.

For a thousand years it had covered the globe with its prospering colonies, its high-turreted garrisons and wide-paved roads, lavish centers of pilgrimage and golden standards of imperial dominance.

The Adamites, a pale-skinned race with red albino eyes and hair so blonde it almost appeared bereft of all color, save for a faint metallic gold tinge, had arrived at the savage lands of Pangaea from the sea, on their dragon-prowed ships.

They came as sea-born gods, clad in gleaming armor made of iron scales and mother-of-pearl. Where the natives of Pangaea greeted them with awe and reverence, they brought a benevolent subjugation, bestowing upon their vassals their art of metallurgy, of mining metals and precious stones and their ingenuity in dominating an as yet pristine and hostile nature.

The Adamites taught the Pangaeans to cultivate the soil, to produce wine from the vine and oil from the olive tree; they taught them to combine herbs and roots to make ecstatic draughts that could break the bonds of mortality and bring man face to face with the gods, outside the realm of space and times.

However, where the natives were hostile towards the newcomers, they soon learned how ineffective their stone spears and obsidian knives were against the iron armor and swords of their conquerors.

The mastery of the Adamites was soon established on Pangaea. Their arts, letters, culture and arms covered the vast expanses of the Pangaea and merged the motley mosaic of its peoples in one massive empire, prospering sometimes under smooth-worded coercion and sometimes under the sting of the slave-driver's whip.

Yet, this thousand-year world order came to pass when dawned a time of cataclysmic upheaval and chaos.

The dark oceans swelled and rose to swallow entire island-continents and earth-rending tremors tore the flesh of Pangaea apart, rending open yawning abysses which were quickly filled with the rushing in of oceanic waves.

Landmasses drifted apart from each other and many a shining city was lost beneath the angry waters. Volcanoes erupted everywhere with such unseen before fury that their plumes of fiery cloud and black fume turned the sky the color of tainted blood.

Twin comets of massive size cruised in the heavens, searing through the massive parapet of the nuclear winter's clouds that hung heavily above all creation.

During daytime they seemed like black

carcinomas, moving and growing at an agonizingly slow speed; at night, they emanated a ghastly pale glow like diabolical moon-gods demanding bloody appeasement.

The chaos of those days was unparalleled. Those cities who had survived the initial onslaught of the tidal waves were gripped by the hysteria of the encroaching end that none could deny.

They collapsed in upon themselves as the torments of the earth grew worse and worse each day. The people turned to their gods in desperation, offering up entire fortunes in gold and ivory and embroidered sea-silks. When their supplications went unanswered, they placed upon the altar their own offspring and reddened the sacrificial troughs with infant blood.

After that, the gates of insanity were flung

wide open.

Some fled to the mountains, seeking refuge in the caves and the inaccessible eyries in high plateaus. Others just turned on one another, in an unbridled and unreasoning frenzy, killing, looting and raping with no thought of tomorrow. Suicide and cannibal cults emerged to prey on those gone insane with fear but were quickly drowned in the red, gore-filled mire overflowing the gutters of the cities.

What vestige of order and law still remained fortified itself in those citadels left standing and fiercely fought off with axe, and stones and burning tar all those who thronged before their gate, regardless of whether they were marauding enemies or honest suppliants of refuge.

No historical record was left of those days to tell how long this time of chaos and brutality lasted.

But when, eventually, all the screaming and the fires subsided, and the comets had sunk below the horizon, never to be seen again, the skies gradually regained their clear blue, the angry waves of the ocean heeled, and the earth was still once more.

The new dawn found nothing but ruins, a Pangaea no longer recognizable, torn to pieces. The empire of the Adamites was in shambles: a globe-spanning graveyard of ruins and sad reminders of past grandeur.

Out of this lamentable landscape scarred by catastrophe, a new power arose. The empire of Nemorensia.

At first, it was nothing more than a coalition between bands of marauders, called the Nemorensian League, determined to pick the bones of a frightened and shattered world clean. But in due time, all wounds heal; and broken bones are set when put long enough into a cast.

The empire of Nemorensia was that cast, and it set the bones of the world according to its whims.

As the initial marauding bands grew in power, the domains they terrorized and extracted tributes from grew far and wide. Gradually, they developed a peculiar form of hypocrisy to go along with their new-found realm of power.

And though they remained cutthroats and slavers at heart, they refined their ways, carved laws into massive monoliths based on a perversion of the old Adamite laws and set themselves up as a legitimate force, destined to maintain peace and order.

They rebuilt the devasted cities near the newly formed coastline and fortified them with high walls of stone in order to prove to their miserable subjects that they no longer needed fear the wrathful ocean stretching out before them.

There were those who said that the gods would punish this hubris of the Nemorensians. But when the gods did no such thing and the prophets of divine retribution were nailed upon T-shaped crosses along the sea, "to keep watch for the coming vengeance of the gods they believed in", it was made evident to everyone on the land that the only thing left to fear in this world was Nemorensian power.

The survivors of the great cataclysm never truly accepted the Nemorensians as their saviors and rulers. They feared them, yes; but at the same time, they realized they needed them in order to survive and prosper and, very soon, people were flocking out of their own free volition to the safe havens and walled cities of the empire.

Thus, it wasn't before long that these swordsmen and raiders acquired the same legitimacy as the lords of old.

Their bands of armed thugs assumed the mantle of an organized armed force and, as their numbers grew exponentially, their exploits were sung as heroic and valiant by the folkish lute and lyre.

Seven hundred years later, the Nemorensian empire had become the established order, steeped in ancient and revered tradition. Its rulers were depicted with the sun-wheel framing their heads and hailed as the saviors of mankind.

The banner of the empire, a great serpent devouring a man who still fought valiantly against the beast with his sword even as he were half-swallowed in its jaws, fluttered on almost every hilltop garrison crowning the vast expanse of land which had once been Pangaea.

The first settlement built by the Nemorensians had grown into a capital city – Naronia.

Its sheer walls of granite rose on the shores of the bay of Iovia and the view from its gleaming spires, tiled with bronze leaf and decorated with hideous basaltic gargoyles, spanned towards the archipelago beyond.

Naronia stood there as a testament of defiance to the watery beast that was the ocean, which had once swept away the Adamite kings and their fabled palaces of enameled brick.

In the course of those seven hundred years, the city of Naronia had already become old and hoary with age, besmeared with the filth that civilization and protected, peaceful lives produce.

Within the center of its colossal walls, situated on a natural craggy elevation, lay the imperial see of the Emperor-Magus in all its extravagant and radiant opulence, towering over the rest of the buildings like a barbarous ornament, heavy with gold and silver and orichalcum inlays.

Seemingly endless hanging gardens surrounded its grounds and atop its tallest spire lay a single massive diamond, the size of an ostrich egg, that had been spewed forth from the convulsing depths of the earth during the era of the great cataclysm. Now it served as symbol of the Emperor's radiance, always filtering the sunlight hitting upon it and creating an artificial rainbow above the entrance of the throne room.

Naronia was known as the *jewel of the empire*, perhaps due to the existence of that enormous jewel in its palace or, perhaps, due to the many lavish public buildings that had been erected in tis aristocratic quarter throughout the centuries.

The rotunda of the senate was a sight to behold, with its massive astrological gear-clock set atop its highest terrace, endlessly marking the rise and the setting of constellations by the tolling of silver bells.

Many bathhouses of porphyrite were to be found everywhere in the city, even amongst the poorest quarters, where whores and peddlers congregated, and business deals were struck by merchants and traders amongst the mists of the sauna rooms where the air was heavy with burning incense.

Pyramid-shaped temples constructed out of

the purest glass towered over the brick-and-mud dwellings of the plebian quarter and through their transparent panes one could see the priests and vestal virgins performing rites before the statues of the dead Nemorensian Emperors and their revered standards which were kept there as holy relics.

Peace reigned throughout the empire. An uneasy, servile peace maintained by a relentless law, always swift to punish.

Thieves would get their hands amputated and runaway slaves their knees sawed off. Adulterous women had their bodies marked all over with a red-hot stamp of iron resembling a pair of lips so as they would be reminded for the rest of their lives the unlawful kisses they had received from their lovers.

Sorcerers, rebels and heretics had their eyes gouged out by ravens bred and trained especially for that form of torture. The eyes, Naronian law dictated, were the gateway to the soul – once that gateway was willfully opened to evil, it could no longer be trusted to remain shut in the future. Therefore, it had to be destroyed.

This law was administered by the Magian cast, a selective and secretive order of loyal servants of the emperor.

These Magi were the only ones allowed to dabble into the arcane art of sorcery, explore the mysteries of nature and experiment with herbs, minerals and animal parts in order to develop cures.

In essence, they were the scientists, mystics and all-around dogma-shapers of the empire, far higher in rank than any priest or state official. And they were all fiercely loyal to the Emperor-Magus who was, after all, one of their own and, at the same time, the head of their order.

They were his eyes and ears in every corner of his realm: sometimes dressed in the full black regalia of their office, distinguished by the raven-feathered crests on their caps, and sometimes disguised as simple folk, they roved far and wide, mingling with the populace, always watching, recording and judging. They had the authority to dispense justice at whim and their rulings could only be overturned by an appeal to the Emperor himself.

The shadow of fear hung heavily over the common people who mostly toiled daily in the fields, from sunrise to sunset, or were too busy exercising their craft or trade to make ends meet.

There were also those relatively well-off who treaded lightly upon their good fortune, least the wrong word or association brought them to the attention of the penetrating stare of the Magus Inquisitor.

Nevertheless, peace and order were maintained. The fields kept yielding forth rich crops, the roads were busy with trading caravans, the bricklayer's and the smelter's furnace never ceased to give off smoke and Naronia's harbor was crowded with fishing and trading vessels.

If the price for this prosperity was to keep one's head down when imperial patrols were passing by and to chose one's words very carefully when drinking at the tavern with strangers, no one complained about it. At least, not openly.

Indeed, very few dared oppose imperial power and those who did always were cautious never to reveal themselves or declare open war against the despotic might of Nemorensia.

Long centuries of oppression had banded together all these rebel souls into an underground secret society of assassins: men and women from the lower tiers of society, trained to operate from within the shadows and always keep their mouths shut even under the most dire distress of torture.

Captured assassins would sooner bite off their own tongues and spit it at the face of the interrogating Magus than give up their brethren-in-the-shadow. They called themselves the Orican Brotherhood, although the designation given to them by their enemies, that of assassins, was the one that had finally prevailed to the common mind – and the Brotherhood had embraced it with a sneer of arrogance.

Assassins were rumored to be the avengers of the common people against the indiscretions of the nobles; yet there were in no way bleeding hearts. If someone wished to hire their services, it cost a pretty penny. Often, a distraught man at the end of his wits, trampled down by the imperial boot of high taxation and cruelty, with nothing left to lose and nothing to pay with, would offer up his own life to the Brotherhood, serving them as a vassal or agent: a deal which the assassins were all too happy to accept.

The Orcian Brotherhood hated vehemently everything that the Nemorensian empire stood for. Whenever their agents would kill, steal or commit arson, it was always for the purpose of weakening the empire or, at the very least, challenging the all-powerful image of authority that the Emperor wanted to put forth to the world. Deceit, subterfuge and sabotage were the Brotherhood's tools just as the poison and the knife. No antiquated sense of honor held them back from obtaining their goals.

But above all, they hated the order of the Magi, whom they viewed as their sworn enemies. Once, assassins had managed to put to the sword an entire contingent of twelve Magi who were on route to a conclave to the Hermitage of Mesimer, in the mountain ranges of the North.

This decimating victory, although erased from the annals of the empire and forbidden by law to be talked about by the people, was still whispered amongst the circles of rebel sympathizers as solid proof that the Magi could bleed and die just like any other man.

II

OF GODS, OLD AND NEW

When the first Emperor-Magus sat on the throne of Nemorensia, he declared that the old gods were dead.

They had abandoned mankind in its hour of direst need and, therefore, any man wishing to call himself sane had to turn his back on them and abandon the worship at their useless and mute altars.

The great cataclysm that had shattered Pangea was solid proof that the old gods were uncaring and cruel celestial sadists.

What few vestiges of their temples had survived the devastation were pulled down by oxen amidst the clamor of blasphemous cries uttered by the agents of the empire. In the rare cases where a holy edifice had remained relatively intact, the

Emperor-Magus decreed that it should be repurposed, no longer to serve as a place of worship, but as imperial property.

The tallest belfry of the once cyclopean temple of Dagon, the scaled god of the vast deep, was converted into a heavily fortified lighthouse-garrison, destined to guide ships into the harbor of Naronia and, at the same time, to keep a watchful eye on the Iovian archipelago and light warning beacons when sea-raiders were seen approaching.

The glass pyramids of the imperial cult sprung up like mushrooms throughout the land where the old temples had once stood and hymns in praise of the salutary might of the Emperor resounded in their daily and nightly rites.

Way-shrines of porphyrite were erected in honor of the fallen heroes of the empire – most of whom were nothing but degenerate warlords who, in life, had killed as indiscriminately as the old gods and thus, in death, enjoyed the same status of divinity.

This coercive new dogma was respected throughout Nemorensia and it expanded as the empire's dominion expanded.

But the hearts of the simple, superstitious folk were not so easy to conquer. There still remained ancient shrines that nature had lovingly concealed in its bosom and the negligence of the imperial agents had not touched.

People yet visited the sacred groves of old at night, despite their fear of being caught and charged with heresy – a crime equal to treason. There, they made offerings of what little they had and implored the old gods to hasten their return to earth once more so that the purging of the Nemorensian tyranny could finally begin by their grace.

No one knew exactly how many were those still faithful to the old gods, for they hid their belief under the strictest discipline of secrecy. The Magi argued that they were but an insignificant handful; and yet they were constantly seeking them out, trying to extract a confession of heresy either through torture or sweet-spoken mind manipulation.

Old timers, well-versed in the ancient lore of the era before the cataclysm, maintained that the kingdom of the old gods was not of this earth. They believed that during the time of the great upheaval the primordial gods had sought refuge in Irkala Kar, the Underworld, and there they were entrapped, destined to serve as the wardens of its horrors and abominations.

They no longer offered solace and material

blessings under the sun, but they were the protectors of the dead, separating the torturers from the tortured in the afterlife and making sure that each individual got their dues for all eternity.

    Was that not justice of a more substantial and sublime kind than any man or woman, persecuted and run down by the despotism of the empire, could ever hope for?

III

ATHANOR'S RUIN

Athanor sat atop a small dune overlooking the beach and listened to the monotonous swooshing of the waves washing ashore.

His brooding gaze wandered off towards the open horizon where he could barely make out the jagged outline of the Isle of Os.

His fishing net was spread all around him and he had part of it propped up on his knee. But he was only pretending to mend it, out of force of sheer habit.

In truth, his mind was too numb to bid his fingers to any actual work.

Even though Athanor was a young man of twenty-six winters, in his prime, that day he looked old and weary beyond his years.

His auburn hair fell to his shoulders in a matted mess of dreadlocks decorated with coral beads. The glimmer in his green eyes was dulled and the deep lines furrowing across his forehead bespoke of a bitter inner struggle going on.

That afternoon, Athanor had realized that his world was coming undone. Not that it was much of a world, anyway; but it was all he had ever known, and he clung to it fiercely.

It was one of those abrupt and numbing realizations which come uninvited and bear with them the dread assurance of being inevitable. Athanor was a simple man – a fisherman, the son of a fisherman.

He had married when he was young, barely out of puberty, a girl he hardly knew; and she had borne him twin daughters. He had grown to love that woman with that ardent, possessive love men have for their hometown when they have never travelled abroad or seen what else the world holds.

Athanor did not ask much from life. Just food on his table, his woman by his bedside every night and the agents of the empire away from his doorstep. And yet, he had been denied even of that little he ever asked for.

Some nosy crone in the village had told him that a fortnight ago she had seen his wife in the market of the nearby town.

She was talking to one of those so-called *sea-lovers*, a mariner from the Isle of Os. They were both laughing, the story went, and this man offered Athanor's wife a necklace made of mother of pearl. Not only she had accepted it, but she also let the man gently fasten it around her neck.

"I may be old", the crone nodded gravely, "but I'm not *too* old to know what your woman's hips meant when they pressed against that necklace-gifting brute".

And just like that, Athanor's fickle illusion of happiness had been dashed down the dark precipice of all-consuming jealously.

The *sea-lovers* from the Isle of Os were a peculiar sort of people. Black-haired and tan, with fierce dark eyes. They always bore an ornate dagger of obsidian in the colorful sashes around their waist. They were quick to draw that blade in anger over trivial matters or when they felt their honor was at stake.

Everyone knew them as traders, travelling merchants and procurers of commodities for those seeking rare or illegal items. Decent folk, that is people long used to bowing their head to the empire's decrees, called them pirates and smugglers.

The empire of Nemorensia had repeatedly tried to conquer the little Isle of Os, off the coast of the gulf of Iovia. Yet surprisingly, their continuous efforts had not proven successful. For though the empire was a force to be reckoned with on land, their fleet was more for show than for anything else.

Besides, a strangle peculiarity seemed to defend the Isle of Os from any would-be invaders.

The entire island was surrounded by jagged volcanic reefs, rising out of the ocean floor and surrounding Os like so many rows of shark-jaws. Its coasts were practically impregnable by anyone who did not know the narrow pathways to navigate through that treacherous sea filled with basaltic spikes.

Therefore, the empire had given up on trying to subjugate that inconsequential little piece of rock in the middle of the archipelago and an uneasy truce existed between the Nemorensians and the Osians.

Still, Osians were allowed to trade in the ports and cities of the empire because their land was rich in amber, a commodity the Nemorensian mages in particular valued highly.

At that moment, Athanor wished the whole damn island had been sunken back into the sea during the great cataclysm.

His eyes narrowed as he gazed towards the open sea and his fingers frantically pulled on the strings of his net, severing the strands instead of mending them.

At first, he didn't want to believe what the crone had told him about his wife, but in his heart, he knew it was real.

For some time, he had sensed that his wife had been growing distant and cold. Her affections, in the rare occasions she conceded to display them, seemed to him somehow detached and forced, more dutiful than loving.

And yet he refused to believe the worse and chose to think that she was in one of her moods.

But when the agents of the empire came knocking at his door that morning, asking the whereabouts of his wife he was convinced that something sinister was afoot.

They said they wanted to question her about her affiliation with an Osian.

Athanor's wife was not at home then. She had risen early and said she would be gone to the faire in the nearby city.

A bitter lump had been stuck in Athanor's throat as he went about his day, moved rather by force of habit than actual will.

He had sailed out with his boat, but he did not have a mind to even cast his nets. He just spent most the day looking at the calm, dark blue of the sea and not uttering a word.

When he finally came back, he did not have the stomach to return home. Instead, he found his way to a remote cove, a good distance from the village, and stayed there, pretending to be mending his nets.

His mind was ablaze with thoughts of anger and betrayal. How could she do this to him?

Happiness was not a complicated thing, in his mind. Why would she go and ruin the perfect and simple happiness they had? What more could she want from life that he couldn't give her? Was there some evil sorcery afoot emanating from that cutthroat's dark eyes which had perverted and twisted her mind?

It was well within his right as a husband to have her thrown out of their home and publicly shamed. And perhaps he would do that; the whore deserved no less.

Then again, Athanor thought of their twin daughters. They would not understand such cruelty and how could he ever explain to them what their mother had done to him?

Perhaps it would be best if something were to happen to her; maybe, an accident. He could take her fishing with him one day and make sure she never returned ashore and then he would be just another grieving husband, struck down by Fate like so many others.

Athanor felt disgusted and ashamed to entertain such violent thoughts. He was not a violent man by nature, but for the first time in his life he felt that he could be one.

But those were just the fancies of a hurt and grieving man, weren't they? Because, at the same time, he loved his wife, and he did not wish to see her come to any harm.

The sun was beginning to set behind the horizon. It was time to head home, anyway. He quickly bundled up his tangled nets, slung them over his shoulder and took the path towards home.

Perhaps he could just confront her, demand answers for what she had done. Yes, this could all be resolved between them. She would fall to her knees, apologize to him and he would be magnanimous enough to forgive her, for the sake of the twins. Without a doubt, that would be the best way to handle the matter, wouldn't it?

He traced his steps back towards the village in the deepening twilight while entertaining such self-righteous fantasies to relieve the confused anguish of his bruised ego.

Perhaps he could slap her around, once or twice, is she gave him lip about the whole thing. Yes, that would do the trick. He just had to show her who was the man of the house.

He was somewhat ashamed to be thinking things like that but, at the same time, he could not deny that they gave him a peculiar sort of satisfaction.

As he approached the village over the sandy dunes, strewn with sea daffodils, he immediately realized something was amiss.

Over the Eastern horizon the sky was hued unnaturally with a tinge of orange and red. At first, he thought it was only some trick of light, some peculiar reflection of the sunset in the West, but as he approached closer, he saw what it truly was. The blaze of a fire. His nostrils stung with the acrid smell of burning wood and hay.

Athanor froze. He dropped his bundle to the ground and started running like a madman towards the village.

As he got closer, he saw the flames' angry glare grow brighter and redder, like blazing embers. His mind went blank. He stumbled and fell and cut his forehead on a sharp stone. But he got up and kept running, gasping for breath, his arms flailing madly.

The entire village had been turned into an

inferno. The straw-thatched huts were blazing like makeshift torches for the winter solstice ceremony.

All around the mud-strewn main street his neighbors and friends, people he knew and those he despised, lay dead and silent. Their faces scorched, their eyes staring, and their teeth exposed in convoluted grimaces of frozen agony.

The women had torn clothes and the red marks of rape upon their bodies. Some were stabbed, others eviscerated and others… well, others were missing their entire faces by the stroke of an axe.

"No, no, no", Athanor stammered in a numb tone. "No, gods! No, no, no!"

Trembling like a man caught in the coils of the giant electric eel that prowled the nearby waters, Athanor's eyes darted from corpse to corpse, trying to find his wife and children amongst the dead, hoping that he would not find them there, yet dreading that he would.

Inadvertently, his dazed steps led him to his own house, a hut among the huts, already burnt down to a cinder.

There lay his wife's body, propped up on the dinner table, her legs still spread, her dress torn to shreds, her faced bashed in beyond recognition.

Spears had been driven through the fragile little bodies of his daughters, impaling the right in their cribs, where they slept warmly blanketed by their own pooling blood.

Athanor's face contorted in a mask of agony. He tried to scream and cry at the same time, but no sound would come out.

He collapsed to his knees and that fragment of a second it took him to hit the ground seemed like an eternity. Tears were streaming down his eyes unchecked. When sound finally managed to come out of his mouth, it was the long, tortured and high-pitched scream of a mind and a heart breaking at the same time.

And all around him, the thick smoke of the burning and the pungent stench of fresh death rose in a black cloud that enveloped the sky and erased the evening star overhead.

IV

THE KING IN THE FOREST

News of the burning of Athanor's village were hardly news in the greater scheme of the things of the Nemorensian empire.

Three months after the destruction, everyone had forgotten all about it and it was as if it had never happened.

Some said it was the empire who had been behind the massacre. The regional Magi had information that locals were cavorting with Osian pirates and harboring 'rebellious thoughts'.

Thus, they decided to send a clear message to what happen to those who chose to defy the empire and lean towards its enemies.

Others said that it was the Osian pirates who did it, because frankly, that was exactly what pirates did. According to that take of events, an Osian pirate had gotten close to a local woman, learned from her about the wealth of the locals, the frequency of imperial patrols and, when the time was right, he decided to put all that information to good use and raid the village dry, for all it was worth.

In either case, it was just another tragedy in an already harsh and cruel world, and no one could be bothered much about it.

Tragic news of that ilk was never discussed around the hearth or in the common rooms of taverns. Those essentially unaffected by them were just grateful to have been spared and chose to dwell on the sweeter savor of life rather than regurgitate tales of senseless death and destruction.

Even Athanor found himself not caring in a very short while. After what he had witnessed, he had cried himself to the point where his eyes were swollen shut and he had slept amidst the ashes of his home until he had lost all sense of time.

Early one morning, compelled by hunger and exhaustion, he finally got up and staggered away without ever looking back, without speaking a word and without shedding another tear.

He was like a drunken man or one of those lost souls who spent their days breathing in the intoxicating fumes of the crimson poppy.

For many long months he wandered from town to town, a man with no name, who scarcely spoke a word. When asked who he was and whence he came, he would shake his head and reply:

"I'm nothing. I come from nothing".

He worked hard at any job he could find, unhesitatingly volunteering to take up even the most arduous and dangerous tasks, with cold abandon.

He labored on the fields and in the mines, herding hogs in the marshes and diving for pearls and sponges until blood trickled out of his ears. And all the coin he earned he would spend on wine and pipefuls of crimson poppy.

It was in one of those dens of fugue from reality that he first heard about the old gods and their miraculous powers.

An old man, his brow beaded with heavy sweat, lay thrashing and raving in his cot, caught in the throes of his delirium.

"They didn't believe me, but I saw it, I saw it! The land beyond all lands, where the gods are in exile. That's where they keep the dead, yes, they do, those jealous bastards! I thought I could get them back and I almost did, you know. It's a burglar's job, breaking in…"

"Get what back?" Athanor had asked offhand, since the drug had not yet fully taken effect on him.

"My boys", the old man sobbed. "The plague took them, my sweet boys… but I've always seen them, you know. Yes, I've always known they were there, just beyond the veil, every time I left offerings on their graves".

Athanor had looked at the raving man with horror and disgust. Was that what his own future looked like? Was he going to become like that or was he already but a younger version of that filthy, raving old man?

Both of them soon sunk into the consoling and absurd visions of the crimson poppy and spoke no more of such things.

Yet when they came to once more, they found themselves exiting that den of shattered dreams and ragged hopes together.

A strange feeling kept nagging Athanor – the absurd thought that there was something more to the old man's words than simply insane ramblings and fantasies.

They made their way to a courtyard where a wine-cart served as an open-air tavern for field-laborers, beggars, and errand swindlers.

There, they wetted their dehydrated lips and got to talking in a secluded corner choked with decomposing garbage.

The old man admitted that he had heard stories of an ancient shrine in the East, located in the midst of a grove which had once been sacred to the hunting goddess of Pangaea.

Thence, as legend had it, mortals could enter into the Underworld and meet again those who they had loved in life.

The priest ministering to that shrine was said to hold the power to lift the veil separating the two worlds, that of the living and that of the dead, yet he never publicly revealed this secret, as far as anyone knew.

The old man shook his head bitterly, saying that the priest had deceived him. When he had asked of him to enter into the Underworld, to visit his sons, the priest had given him a map. But the map was all wrong. It had led him into a cave, a dank and dismal place strewn with fragments of ancient bones, and all he had found there was silence and misery. No passage to the world beyond lay there, no ancient secrets revealed – nothing at all.

"It's all a sham, I'm afraid, my boy", he said bitterly. "Forgive me for blabbering about it as if it were true, while I was under the poppy's thumb. The old gods were cruel back then and they are still cruel now, playing upon our fears and hopes, them sons of celestial bitches. Once someone is gone, they're gone for good. You'd best forget all such poppycock and get on with your life, if you can. You hear me?"

Athanor nodded and bade the old man goodbye. In truth, he wasn't. He became fixated with the old man's story and spent the rest of his days asking as many people as he could the way to that forest shrine in the East.

Most were reluctant to tell him, fearing that he was an agent of the empire or a spy for the Magi, trying to root out believers in the old ways.

Yet, some gentle souls along the way really

saw the pain and desperation in his eyes and told him what they knew, pieced together from vague travelers' accounts or urban legends they had heard.

Thus, Athanor began travelling towards the East, always headed for areas where the oaks were ancient and grew tall upon the waving hills; ever asking about the old gods, the keepers of those trapped in the dismal Below.

He wandered far, and he walked on nights without end. Sometimes the dawn found him half dead from fatigue by the side of the road, for he travelled like a desperate man driven forward only by the sheer force of a hope beyond hope.

Then, one night when the hunting moon was waxing full, Athanor found himself out into the wild, surrounded by the living pillars of a sylvan cathedral of oaks.

He had no idea if he were in the right grove or not, but he kept stumbling on nevertheless, as he had done for more days than he could count at that point.

Suddenly, his weary, blood-shot eyes fell upon the man. A crooked and bent figure, sat on his haunches in the midst of a clearing, bathed in the sickly ochre glow shed forth upon the earth by the moon. He was an emaciated man with thin strands of white hair clinging to his liver spotted skull and grasping tightly a crescent-bladed scissor in his right hand. His eyes ever darted back and forth, like those of a hunted animal, and his lips were constantly moving, mumbling inaudible formulae and mantras.

Athanor felt a fluttering inside his stomach. He realized that this must be the minister of the forest shrine, the keeper of the way to the Underworld. A spark of hope ignited in his heart. But it was grim hope, saturated with the fear of denial and failure.

Nevertheless, he mustered what courage and physical strength was left in him to approach the old priest in the moonlight, extending his left hand forward as a token of his peaceful intentions. He opened his mouth to voice a reverential greeting, but he did not have time to utter it.

With a shrill, guttural cry the gaunt man lounged at him, snarling like a rabid dog.

"So, you think you're the one? You think you can do it better than me, eh? I'll show you better. I'll show you your insides!" he cried.

Athanor was completely taken aback. He had precious little time to react. The priest fell upon him like a mangy, famished dog swooping down hungrily on a pile of freshly discarded leftovers from the table.

He felt the old priest's bony fingers grip his throat like a vice and the piercing sting of his curved blade slice across his forehead.

Stifling a cry of surprised anguish, Athanor fought back with all he had. He kicked and punched and shoved, trying to get that animated corpse of a man off him. They both stumbled and fell on the ground grunting.

Athanor tried to crawl away, but the old priest, moving with unnatural agility, was upon him once more, straddling his back and bringing down his scissor, trying to cut through his ribs.

Athanor screamed in pain. Even as he did, his fingers closed around something hard and jagged: a stone. Without thinking, he took hold of it and turning around smashed the priest in the face with it.

With a screech of pain, the old man fell back,

and his blade flew out of his grasp. Athanor, incensed by the rush of adrenaline from his wounds, did not hesitate. He smashed the priest again with the rock and grabbing the discarded blade he ran it across his wrinkled throat, opening it wide open and letting forth a spray of steaming red blood.

For a brief instant, a terrible lucidity flashed across the priest's eyes, a split second before all life spilled out of him in the diminishing gush of the gory fountain Athanor had opened.

"Thank you", he wheezed horribly through his half-severed trachea and bloody bubbles oozed forth from the fatal wound.

Athanor lay there, alone once more in the night, panting and bleeding. The scissor was in his hand, drenched with gore. What had he done? His mind was swirling. He had come to that grove looking for answers, for a glimmer of hope, and instead all he had found was more insanity, more death.

He slowly collapsed on the moist sylvan floor and lay there, upon his back, looking up at the grinning face in the moon as the adrenaline rush of the past few moments came crashing down, turning into exhausting lethargy.

His eyes closed against his will and he slipped into a sleep full of merciless dreams.

V

BERYL EYES

Athanor was awakened by the sound of chiming bells and the soft whisper of melodies uttered through feminine lips.

He opened his eyes, wiped the cackled blood from his forehead and sat up. The hunting moon was at its zenith, seta against the black, star-spattered skies overhead. He could see it glimmering like a glaring predator's eye through the foliage of the oaks.

Once again, he heard that distant song of women, this time much closer than before and knew it then to be real, and not a hallucination of his strained mind.

He quickly jumped to his feet and grasped the scissor blade, turning around wildly, his weapon stretched out in challenge. Yet all he could see were the moonbeams dancing on the forest floor.

And then, suddenly, those moonbeams seemed to come alive and take human form. Their pure silver glow crystalized into the beauty of seven sylph-like feminine forms, clad in transparent silken robes.

Their long, flowing hair was like a sheet of fallen autumn leaves. Some were golden-haired, while others had a fire red or auburn mane. But their eyes! Their eyes were as clear as the moon itself, radiant and full of mysteries.

Their dainty feet seemed to glide over the decomposing foliage on the ground, barely touching it, as they approached Athanor from all sides.

He did not know how to react. He had never seen a sight more beautiful in his life, and yet, his bewildered senses warned him of some lurking menace.

The arms of the women stretched out and touched him comfortingly, caressing him and pulling him closer to their lithe bodies. Their lips uttered mesmerizing, hypnotic words in a language that his mind could not comprehend but his heart seemed to know already.

Their kisses covered him like a stupefying surge of electricity.

At that moment, Athanor did not ask the why and the how. It seemed to him that he had strayed into a bizarre, erotic dream, and all he could do was completely surrendered to it.

Everything was a haze of kisses, heaving breasts and enflamed loins straddling him; hands pushed him down and tore his clothes away. He felt the velvet flesh of those sylphs pressing against him, oddly cold. And he completely yielded to the numbing sensation of those otherworldly caresses.

As the fires of passion burned brighter and brighter, so grew the violence of the women's kisses.

At first, it started as pleasurable little nibbling on his lips, a pinch on his nipples; but as the hunting moon glowed ever more fierce overhead, so these sylphs built up their frenzy, transforming into maenads.

Their nails dug into Athanor's flesh and he gasped. Their rosy lips bit him so hard they drew blood. He tried to push them off, but they forced him down, holding him there, like a massive weight made of flowing white silk and supple flesh.

As the others held his arms and legs down, a redhead reached and caressed his face and then drove her thumbs into his sockets. Athanor screamed and the forest echoed with his resounding agony. He could feel warm blood gushing over his cheeks and trickling down like burning tears.

He felt strangely betrayed at that moment, for he had promised to himself that he would never cry again – and yet there he was, shedding his last tears, even though they were crimson and involuntary.

He struggled and screamed but it was all in vain. He heard the sickening sound of his own eyeballs being torn out of his skull. What a shameful way to go, he thought. Blind and with an erection that refused to subside.

A redheaded sylph with glowing eyes made an awful regurgitating sound. Her stomach swelled and heaved unnaturally, as if she were fighting to give birth or summon forth something from her insides.

She reached into her mouth and took out two large beryl stones, almond shaped like human eyes, and forced them into Athanor's gored sockets.

"Let him see, Hunting Mother", she cried out to the moon, "First let him see with true sight and then we'll make him feel with a true heart, so he may be king!"

She reached to his chest, digging her nails into the flesh, directly over his heart. Athanor was sure what was to follow.

Mustering all his strength, with a piercing scream, he yanked his right arm free and grabbed the scissor lying close by. Without even thinking about it, he began swinging left and right, cleaving at those demonesses, screaming, and snarling murder like a madman.

The women shirked in horror as the curved blade cut into their tender flesh and splattered their white gowns red.

Athanor kept stabbing blindly, for a vast and crushing darkness was consuming him, making him to lash out in all directions. He did not stop hacking even when he could no longer feel any form near him.

He stabbed and slashed and screamed at the air, frothing in the mouth, until he had no more strength left. He collapsed to his knees.

Something magnificent and terrible happened then. He realized he could see. His vision had somehow returned. But it was not any kind of vision known or experienced by mortal man.

He could see the world around him as through a dim crystal. Everything was distorted and askew.

Where trees were before, now he could still make out their shapes but at the same time he could see their ancient, hoary faces, the vegetative life-force coursing through their roots.

Where the ground was, he could now see the cavernous pockets beneath it and the veins of precious metals lining their walls. He could see the animal life-force pulsating like a thing alive, a highway of communication, made of tendrils, extending from the bird sleeping in the bough and connecting it to the lizard lurking beneath the rocks.

It was a world of hidden wonders that had been opened to his beryl eyes – and yet it was alien, menacing and confusing; full of sounds, sensations and colors he never knew existed.

He could see the words whispered by the

wind take almost corporeal form and its whisperings were as alluring as they were incomprehensible and maddening.

As if in a lucid trance, Athanor followed the flowing shades of these words, staggering and jumping at the slightest stir of the leaves – for to his new senses this simple rustling felt like a peal of thunder.

Stumbling through this seething nightmare wonderland the woods had suddenly become, he finally came before the opening of an enormous cave.

He stood there transfixed, gazing at it, watching it yawn, full of jagged granite teeth that trembled as if a beast of stone was roaring in a dimension where time flowed incredibly slow and the opening was destined to close when that roar died out eventually.

"Come, child. Come forward", the wind whispered.

And Athanor obeyed without thinking, stepping into the darkness.

VI

WE, THE BONES

The darkness of the cavern was not dark at all to his new eyes.

It was black, yes, but it was a vibrant blackness, full of tendrils of a still darker shade and the pulsating glow of ore veins running along the stony dome like strands of some metallic, subterranean milky way.

Athanor walked on unsure feet down a downward sloping path and the walls of the cavern kept growing wider apart, at last giving way to an enormous, naturally shaped vault, studded with low-hanging stalactites.

Niches were carved all along the walls of the cavern, starting from the floor and reaching a hundred feet high, well-nigh to the domed ceiling. In each niche a human skull was placed, blackened with long years in the damp blackness and grinning.

It was in that moment that Athanor knew that it was not the voice of the wind he had heard and followed, but the voice of those appalling bones.

And it was then the terrible realization dawned on him that the dead were everywhere in the world, ever whispering obscenities to the living, cajoling them on to join them in their own realm of decay.

It wasn't a flight of his tormented fancy or an irrational assumption; it was something he could clearly see now.

"Come closer, child", the skulls whispered in jumbled voices. "Look on us and see all that mortals can ever be".

Athanor felt a sense of dread wash over him.

The skulls seemed to be everywhere around him, looking down on him, even though they had no eyes to speak of.

"What do you want of me? What is this?" Athanor rasped and his voice resounded hollow within the confines of the cavern.

"This is welcome and goodbye", the bones jeered. "It is time to bid goodbye to all you once knew. Goodbye to the lie. And it is time to welcome the truth".

"The truth?" Athanor echoed.

"The naked truth, yes. Stripped of all pretenses, as it is stripped of the illusion of the flesh. Tell us, child, what do you desire most?"

Athanor's brow furrowed and his lips were drawn to a snarl.

"I want this to be over. I want to be with my

wife again. I want none of this to ever have happened", he admitted.

His tone made it evident that he was fighting to restrain himself. In the end, he finally broke. "I don't want your truth".

The bones laughed and the sound of it was unearthly, piercing and clicking in the air about him like the noise of a gigantic centipede moving unseen.

"But that's all you have. That is your last hope to ever see her again".

Athanor's entire body trembled. His knees could no longer support him, and he fell down, whimpering silently.

Exhaustion tormented his every muscle, and his mind was aflame with a grim bewilderment he had never before experienced, not even at the sight of his devasted village and slaughtered family.

"Tell me, what do you want of me?" he murmured in an almost inaudible whisper.

"The question is what do *you* want of *you*, child" the bones retorted. "Do you want to forever lament what life took from you or do you want to embrace death and there reign as king?"

Athanor did not reply. He dreaded what would come out of his mouth, he feared to hear his own words.

The truth was that he was tired of crying and dying inside little by little. He was tired of loss and that feeling of awful helplessness.

As if in reply to his gut-wrenching feeling, a brilliant flash of light issued forth from the eye sockets of the skulls and, at once, a long series of torches burst into flames at the far end of the cave, illuminating gradually the recesses of a tunnel stretching into the distance.

Athanor gulped and gasped for air, painfully taking a hold of himself once more. He clenched his fists, got up and started walking towards the flickering torchlight.

"Go, child", the bones urged him on. "Your throne of anguish awaits thee".

He entered the tunnel amidst the overlapping whispers and jeers of approbation coming from every direction at once.

The incessant noise these abominable remains were making from their niches, coupled with the cavern's natural echo, appeared to have a mesmerizing effect upon him.

The torchlight was blinding to his beryl eyes and he could see salamanders with bodies made of living fire leaping from the ignited part of the torches onto the walls of the tunnel, silently following him.

He couldn't say how far he had walked for any sense of distance or space, as measured by human senses, was quickly abandoning him. All he knew was that the tunnel ended abruptly in a yawning chasm, darker than the deepest shade of black the human eye could ever perceive.

Athanor stood on the precipice and opened his hands. At that moment it was clear to him what he had to do. He let himself go and plunged into the void.

"Welcome, child. Welcome home", the bones hissed in a cacophony of joy, behind him.

VII

IRKALA KAR

Athanor was falling – falling for what seemed an eternity. At first, his hands flayed out instinctively to reach and grab hold of something, but upon failing to do so, he soon resigned completely to that endless fall through the dense ether.

It was strange that he didn't feel anything – not the rushing of the wind, nor the pull of gravity; nothing at all.

In fact, his perception of time was so distorted that he found himself unable to remember a time when he was not falling.

Thus, when he came to an abrupt halt, it felt like a tremendous shock and a tortured gasp escaped from his lips, as if he were emerging from a great depth of water.

Oddly enough, he found himself on his feet and not sprawled down, as he would have expected.

However, it wasn't so much that he had landed upright on a solid surface as that there was no upright position to speak of.

As he somewhat regained his composure, he realized his was standing once more on the edge of a precipice. He felt as if he hadn't moved at all and yet the scenery all around him was entirely different from the confined blackness of the tunnel.

Something had changed in his vision as well. Things were no longer out of focus and intermingled in a dizzying mess. They were clear and sharp. His beryl eyes seemed to have been made exactly for that strange place he found himself in, designed to fully perceive and take in its otherworldly sights.

His boggled mind, however, was having a

harder time registering all that it was seeing.

Overhead, the sky was all hues of gray, as if perpetually covered by smoke or dust clouds. Here and there, where the greyness parted, he could see morbid shades of purple and crimson.

Was it a sky, though? It was definitely a vast and dome-like space, choke-full of gray smoke, but he could perceive without doubt that beneath it all this dome was crisscrossed with something that looked like lightning frozen in place, or gigantic, vast, celestial veins.

He couldn't tell if he were in an actual place or inside a gargantuan behemoth of a living being. A murkiness was diffused about, making the mere act of looking a strain. It was neither darkness nor light, but rather a perpetual penumbral haze reigned wherever he turned. There was no time in that place.

Only eternity. As far as his eye could see, plains of ashen grey dust stretched to a horizon that was askew and distorted.

The laws of Euclidian geometry did not seem to apply there.

Trees long-dead formed forest on hillsides that were distant yet near; lofty towers, like spikes, crowned seemingly inaccessible mountaintops; ruins mixed with stalagmites formed entire valleys, where artificial and natural formation were all confused and difficult to tell apart which was which; partially demolished staircases seemed to descend from the heavens and ended in mid-air, suspended hundreds of miles above the ground. Paths rolled forward and at the same time backwards, hills extended up and down and inwards. Slopping mountainsides converged into a vast, bottomless crater from whence flames spurted skywards and where an entire forest was ablaze in perpetual combustion.

It was from thence that the thick clouds of grey fumes that masked the sky issued forth and the pulsation of the flames was like the heartbeat of a living thing.

It was a dizzying and maddening sight to behold and yet, despite it all, it stood there clear as day.

Athanor was surprised to realize that it took him only a few moments to adapt to that preternatural geometry and soon his was able to navigate his gaze around.

He looked about him, in his immediate vicinity. Right over the edge of the precipice where he stood he could see a murky river of black oil flowing in serpentine coils and disappearing through irrational turns and twists into what his once human senses would have understood as *the distance*.

Next to that body of bubbling and slushing black ooze, another river branched off. This one was shimmering brilliantly, as if made of congealed oil or, perhaps, volcanic glass, trailing off in an entirely different direction.

At that moment, a strange sense of geometrical harmony comforted Athanor. He was standing on the elevated point of a triangle, he reasoned, and all he had to do was make a choice which side to follow.

Without being able to explain why, he was overwhelmed by a profound knowing that upon reaching either one of the triangle's next points he would be on the right track. The right track to what?

That was something he could not answer but,

at that point, logic as he had known it seemed like a distant childhood dream.

He crouched and flung himself forward in a magnificent leap through the air he would have never dared to execute before.

Sure enough, he landed with a heavy splash on one knee inside the murky river of black oil. He wasn't hurt, just as he knew he wouldn't be. As he began wading through the shallow ooze, he could sense that not only the world around him was imbued with high strangeness, but also something was very odd about his own body.

Yes, it was still his body – but at the same time, it wasn't. It felt like his mortal flesh had wasted away, leaving a blank husk remotely resembling the person he once was. His skin felt bizarrely liquified, his lips and eyelids somehow stuck together. When he tried to open them, long, gooey strands of flesh stretched out hindering the process.

Terrified, with a silent scream drowning in his throat, he grabbed a handful of the dark, oily liquid from the river and rubbed it over his face. To no avail. His semi-liquified flesh did not wash away but only mixed with the blackness of that briny slime.

A muffled groan of terror escaped from the shredded membrane covering his lips as he staggered out of the river, moved by a primitive and powerful instinct of fear.

Dripping with mire and trembling all over with cold shivers of horror, he blindly stumbled towards the path of black volcanic glass.

His feet slid on its surface but, somehow, he managed to remain upright and even use this effect to his advantage, building up a great speed of pace.

What amazed him even through the haze of his bewilderment and mental agony was that he did not feel any pain. He knew his body was deformed and mutilated but, in truth, he did not feel any physical suffering, nor did it seem to hinder his movements and reflexes in any way.

He wandered aimlessly for hours upon the black, volcanic glass until he started relishing the sensation of walking on wavering feet – a sensation akin to gliding.

He had no idea where he was nor where he was headed, and that profound feeling of purposelessness was the closest he had come to happiness in a very long, long time.

The further he walked, looking about him like a bewildered stray animal, the more he realized that there was only one place where he could be:

Irkala Kar, the realm of the Underworld.

Was that it? Was he really dead? Yet, if he were truly dead, why was he so dreadfully conscious of everything? Where was that blissful oblivion the dead were said to enjoy? The bones in the cavern had promised that when he saw 'the truth' he would find his salvation.

And though it was true that he could see more clearly than ever before – even the intertwining, serpentine writhing of all the dimensions that were part of the fabric of reality – he could not see anything remotely resembling salvation in sight.

He kept walking and his course seemed to be without end, for he had no means of measuring distance or the passage of time in a world where no such things existed.

Still, with every step he took he felt a burden

weigh down on him; a burden of madness, a fierce scorching sensation in the back of his mind that ever inflamed an itch of insanity.

It was a vexing sensation which had the taste of fear mixed with shame and the dreadful feeling of being hunted by something unknown and terrible - something which did not want to kill him but torment him between life and unlife, forever gnawing and regurgitating the shreds of his dismembered soul.

Burdened with such thoughts and spurred by terrifying impulses, he suddenly spotted in the distance a great basaltic arched gate looming in the horizon. It was an absurd threshold, leading into the ash-strewn nothingness of the surrounding wasteland. A terrible stench emanated from it, carried by the wind, even from such a great distance.

Athanor approached the arched gate even

though he knew in his heart of hearts that something abominable lurked there and what little sense of his former self remained in him begged him not to take a step further.

His legs were moving seemingly mastered by a will of their own. As he drew nearer, he could make out enormous piles of excrement, rising like gargantuan dung hills from the ground, honeycombed with human remains sticking out of them.

These revolting mounds surrounded the gate and flanked it on either side, like piles of raw material in some junkyard of flesh waiting to be used in some unnatural operation.

Athanor shuddered. He clenched his fists, and it was then that he felt the familiar and reassuring weight of the scissor in his hand.

Even though hadn't noticed it before, he hadn't dropped his weapon all this time – which was very odd; but, at that moment, he was glad he hadn't.

As he entered the narrow corridor leading up to the arch, flanked on either side by towering piles of human excrement and decomposing viscera, the gate towered before him like a colossal threshold of dread.

He thought he heard a faint crawling sound in the distance and turned around abruptly. There was nothing there. He quickened his pace, holding his hand in front of his face to protect himself against the intrusion of the unbearably vile stench.

And then he saw it, emerging from behind one of the piles. It was an unholy creature, standing on two legs like a man malformed, more scarab than human, with is bony insect plates interlaced between patches of human skin. Its jaws were spasmodically opening and closing and its front extremities, those of a scarab beetle, were engaged in the act of pushing a great big ball of slimy feces. An apron of disfigured leather, sewn out of human face-skins, covered most of its body.

Upon seeing Athanor, the creature's antennae grew rigid and keen. It let out a piercing shriek from the depths of its shell. With the enormous power of its insect limbs, it shoved the ball of excrement towards him at a breath-taking speed like a projectile.

Athanor had precious little time to react. The vile ball struck him flat on the chest and disintegrated all around him even as he fell down in a puddle of unspeakable filth.

Before he knew it, the scarab-like monstrosity was upon him and the stench of its jaws was hot upon his face.

Saw-like appendages pinned down Athanor's shoulders and dug into his sides. He screamed and instinctively brought his knees up, pushing the creature away from him. It stumbled back for a moment.

Athanor, acting purely on instinct, sprung to his feet, and lashed out with his crescent blade. The first blows glanced off the scarab-man's plates but then Athanor's bronze found the tender part of human flesh in the creature's thigh and sliced opened what must have been its femoral artery.

A gush of black blood erupted, and the monster shrieked, falling on its back, its hideous legs clawing the air.

He let out a muffled, battle cry of pure frenzy and fell upon it, slashing and hacking away at any exposed spot he could find. Showers of dark blood spattered across his face and body and he did not stop pouncing on his foe until he was sure the deformed thing would move no more.

Athanor's beryl eyes shone with an almost red glow as he drew in breaths in short, sharp rasps.

Everything had happened so fast. He was now just past the threshold of the arched gate, alone amidst the revolting mounds, standing in a pool of the scarab-man's blood.

Clearly, whatever that thing had been, it did not expect to meet any resistance from its victims. That was why, Athanor surmised, it had fallen so easily.

The vast expanses of the Underworld spread all around him in every askew and unnatural direction. A distant wind was whispering, carrying a faint song upon its invisible and unfelt gales:

"Power is never given. It is taken. Take its wings and fly to me".

Athanor was not sure if he was finally going completely insane, or if he had really heard that. But he no longer cared to distinguish between madness and reality. After all, what was the difference, really?

In any case, the voice was right. He turned the corpse of the creature on its face and set down to the grim task of hacking off its scarab-wings, prying them off its shell.

Once finished, he took those grim trophies and gazed at them, uncertain as to what he needed to do next.

Instinctively, he tore off his shirt and reaching back, he placed them against the semi-liquid flesh of his new body. To his horror and ghastly surprise, the wings seemed to come alive and the severed tendons hanging from their root twitched and burrowed into his skin.

An intoxicating sensation of blissful numbness washed over him. For the first time since he had entered that accursed place, he felt some degree of certainty that he was alive; that he was strong.

As the wings gradually took root into his flesh, so did his mind fill with all that the scarab-like abomination had seen and done. Visions flashed across Athanor's brain, visions, and sensations of consuming the delicious bits and pieces of the condemned dead, the alien memories of a sadistic idiot with six, razor-sharp extremities.

Athanor burst out laughing without even fully knowing why. The red glare in his beryl eyes grew brighter. He spread his hands to the membranous, smoke-veiled skies, as if to embrace them. In his right hand he still held fast his scissor, dripping with black gore.

As if moved by the exhilaration of will coursing through his body, the wings he had seized from the monster began to flutter and to stir.

Athanor felt his body being lifted up into the fume-choked heavens and he saw the ground shrink beneath his feet. He kept laughing at the sheer delight of the sight, like a madman drunk with new-found vice, and fixed his stare to the far horizon.

He could see the black basaltic path he had followed trail off through ragged hills and looming ruins, like a frozen trickling tear. Through the veils of perpetual twilight diffused about he surveyed the landscape far and wide from his high vantage point and could make out where other three arched gates loomed along the banks of the glassy river.

What deformed monstrosities guarded them? No, that was not the important question. What secrets and what twisted delights did they hold, if he reached out violently enough to claim them?

With a mighty thrust of his entire body and a loud buzzing of his newly acquired wings he darted forth through the rank air, spiraling through dimensions askew, and made his way deeper into Irkala Kar, without realizing or caring he had just become a little more demon and a little less man.

VIII

THE PENUMBRAL MAN

Flying through the quiet and vast heavens of the Underworld, Athanor felt like a fetus swimming around its mother's womb. And indeed, he wasn't so much flying as he was swimming, slushing really, through the shifting ether.

A crimson-gold glare in the distance caught his eye, coming from within the black outline of a bulky structure on the ground below that looked like a tortoise's shell, surrounded by half a dozen towers giving off thick plumes of smoke. It looked like a workshop or foundry of sorts. Nearby, another one of those arched gates of shimmering basalt stood, forbidding and ominous.

Athanor grinned, and his semi-liquified lips stretched to reveal unnaturally his teeth up to the back of his jawbone. He swooped down and landed effortlessly before the gate.

Acrid smoke invaded his nostrils and made his eyes water as he approached the tortoise-shell structure. The clamor of metal on metal rang deafeningly to his ears in an unmistakably keen and clear tone. He could make out the glow of a large furnace in the interior of the building and a slumped figure working over an anvil, pounding away at something which gave off alternately metallic clangs and wet, thumping sounds alike.

Athanor gripped his scissor in anticipation. As silently as he could, he entered the workshop and closed in on the artificer at the forge. He was almost at stabbing distance when he took his final cautious step forward.

It was then that he felt a trip wire snap with a

barely audible twang. Immediately, a steam whistle blurted out its piercing scream and the figure on anvil turned around to face the intruder.

An inhuman grin, half made of scrap metal and half of ragged flesh, greeted Athanor.

The artificer at the forge was a creature resembling a mix between a corpse and a crude machine. Chains held its limbs in place, supporting them to a metallic apparatus of turning gears and cogs; and its right hand was shaped like an enormous hammer: a mesh of barbed wire was wrung tightly from the creature's shoulder, reaching down all the way to its arm, which ended in a cluster of innumerable severed human fists, frozen by rigor mortis in the act of clenching, held together by barbwire so as to form a hammer-shaped appendage, disproportionately large to the rest of the creature's form.

"Ah, another meat-sack", the monstrosity growled in glee. "Give me your spare parts, meat-sack".

Athanor's eyes narrowed. The time for awe-struck hesitation was past.

He bent his knees and leaned forward, assuming a fighting position. Even as the creature lounged at him, raising its hammer arm to strike, he leapt into the air and somersaulted behind the beast of flesh and metal, landing with his blade extended outwards and slashing a deep gash between its shoulder blades.

Sparks flew as his scissor cut through flesh but found only bones of iron underneath.

The monster laughed a sickening snarl and turned to grip Athanor by the throat, threatening to crush his windpipe.

"Now I'll fix you up for judgement good", it cackled.

Athanor did not know what that meant, nor did he particularly care to find out.

Instead of trying to fight off the beast's grip he took hold of its swollen wrists, planted his legs firmly down and pushed himself into the air, flapping his scarab wings with all his might.

The monster seemed momentarily startled by that move but held fast. Athanor, even as he choked and gasped for breath in the creature's grip, kept struggling to gain as much height as he could, dragging the hulking abomination in the air with him.

He fought with every ounce of strength in his body for every foot he rose towards the foundry's domed ceiling, directly above an open smelting crucible of gigantic proportions.

Wheezing and rasping as life's dear breath was squeezed out of him, he desperately took to hacking and slashing at the creature's arm wrapped around his neck.

The first blow severed tendons and struck against metallic bones. The second, however, was so strong that Athanor's scissor shattered; yet, in doing so, he managed to break the control of the creature's death-grip.

With nothing to hold on to, the deformed artificer plummeted down and with a searing splash landed inside the crucible's mass of molten, flaming metal.

The creature let out a piercing cry of agony as its flesh began to melt away and its metal parts were dissolved into the fires it had kindled itself.

Athanor landed back down, out of breath and rasping heavily. His weapon was useless, and the fury of his final blow had driven the handle of the scissor so deep into his own flesh that his hand was bleeding profusely.

In a fit of rage, he threw the broken weapon into the smelter, striking the head of the creature – its only part remaining still unconsumed by the slushing ripples of molten metal.

Throughout its slow and excruciatingly painful death, consciousness and terrible awareness glimmered in its eyes, even when its mouth had been submerged and its screams no longer had a mouth to issue from.

Once the creature's monstrous life was snuffed, Athanor relaxed his tense muscles and stood upright, examining his surroundings more closely.

The walls were lined with shelves packed with bizarre metal parts made of bronze and copper and orichalcum. Large baskets full of severed human limbs were stacked near an infernal apparatus that looked like a gigantic sewing machine which used wire instead of thread. A variety of projects, some completed, some half-finished, were laid in a row on a large table of ebony. Some were pieces of strange machinery, while others looked like simple tools and weapons.

Athanor was drawn towards one of these, a great sword hanging on a wall plate on its own. It was made of blackened orichalcum and had human bone handle for two hands. Its double edge was like a saw, resembling rows of shark teeth.

He picked it up and weighted it in his palm. It was surprisingly light and perfectly balanced. He swung it around, relishing the sound the blade made as it swooshed through the air.

His dripping grin spread across his face. A desire for carnage seemed to sip from the sword's handle and into him in an intoxicating flow of slaughter-filled fantasies that flashed across his mind.

Athanor cackled silently and the fires from the furnaces of the foundry cast nightmarish dancing shadows across his features. His beryl eyes grew even redder in glow and as the scorched carcass of the artificer finally sank underneath the molten metal in the crucible all of the creature's knowledge flooded into him and merged with his own memories in a subtle osmosis.

He could now *remember* how to sever sinew from bone with surgical precision, even though he never had that knowledge in the first place; and he could *remember* replacing the living parts of the human body for mechanical ones, better, more durable, more well-suited to the purification of the soul.

He now knew this to be a necessary procedure of preparation for the final judgment awaiting all those who entered the Underworld.

And yet, at the same time, he knew also that such rituals were for the weak, for the sheep. He was a wolf and, possessing the knowledge he did, would never freely acquiesce to submit to such torments and humiliations.

Athanor emerged from the artificer's workshop a changed man – if man he still was. He breathed in the fetid air and sighed in exhilaration, with a newfound appetite for bloodshed.

****

The pathway of black volcanic glass, wherein nothing was reflected, stretched on for miles and miles – at least, that was the best way words could describe its length, since in Irkala Kar measuring distance lost all conventional meaning.

Athanor knew that he should be feeling tired from his endless and ceaseless wandering, but in a place where no time existed physical fatigue also became a thing utterly relative.

Everything seemed to happen rapidly and, simultaneously, with the slow pace of eternity.

Events flowed by with the loose cohesion of a nightmare – a nightmare without end; a nightmare which kept convincing Athanor to give in and enjoy the ride.

In truth, his gradual giving in was the

equivalent of fatigue. And the more he gave in, the more of his former humanity he gave up.

During his long and arduous wanderings, he crossed two more arched gates. In each of them, he faced another terror and emerged victorious, steeped in stinking, unnatural blood. And each time he was laughing even harder than the last.

Both guardians spoke of the judgment awaiting him, in cryptic terms intended to intimidate him. But he made sure their boastful words were abruptly hushed out in a gurgle as he sliced open their throats with the jagged teeth of his blade.

Athanor was not ready to yield to the whims of any abomination seeking to judge him. His great two-handed sword flashed in the dim light and a torrent of blood erupted at his every blow.

From each of his fallen foes he would rip a

bloody trophy with his orichalcum blade and then continue on his way.

At the third gate, he put to the sword a despicable thing resembling a spider cross-bred with a woman. From its eviscerated belly, he pulled a net made of slime and strangled the monster's deformed offspring with it. He decided to keep it, realizing that the mucus-like substance forming it was hard as iron and yet flexible as heated wax.

At the fourth gate, he slaughtered a pale-skinned giant, living inside the stinking husk of a gargantuan crab. Out of the beast's hoary skin he cut plates of crab-shell fused with the giant's muscles and he fashioned a dripping, bony cuirass for himself.

Just like its predecessor, the giant expired gurgling that there was no escaping the final judgement.

Athanor didn't care. He was growing weary of these nonsensical and cryptic aphorisms. They sounded too priestly – too empty. Besides, with each victory he lost a little more of his humanity and saw the world through the eyes of the horrors he had faced and defeated. The thrill of the kill did not sustain him for long. It grew stale and tasteless to his soul. The twisted ugliness of the Underworld was beginning to make him sick to the core of his being. He abhorred that constant sensation of impending dread that he seemed to breathe in at every inhalation.

It wasn't before long – or, perhaps, it was an eternity later – that he began to long for the world above, even with all its poignant miseries.

What a paradise the cruelties of the

Nemorensian empire seemed to him at that moment! He longed for the touch of sunlight, for the caress of fresh air upon a skin that would be solid; he yearned to see again the places where he had once been happy — even if only to remember how they looked.

But there seemed to be no end to that crimson-vaulted hell wherein he wandered. Despair began to creep into his heart. And after that, resignation came to him as naturally as breath.

He did not even flinch when he came across a malformed behemoth chained to a crag upon a narrow mountain pass. The gargantuan ogre was leashed to the living rock by iron hooks piercing the flesh of its back and causing it perpetual agony and rage.

The clash was brief. Athanor's blade swung true and cut deep. He did not laugh as he butchered the beast. He did not even think.

Collapsing next to the shredded corpse, he gazed blankly at his red hands, bathed in gore as they were.

His entire body felt like a sore, festering wound. Was it from the struggle of the fight? Because he still couldn't feel any pain; at least not pain in any corporeal sense. Though, for the first time since entering Irkala Kar, he felt the need to lie down and rest.

It wasn't so much a physical need, as much as a fervent desire to imitate something of his former life, a desperate attempt to feel human again.

But no rest came to him. His mind buzzed with thoughts that were not his own. His limbs twitched with desires that were alien to him.

It took significant effort to get up again, using

his great sword as a crutch. He dragged his footsteps uphill, wandering aimlessly. Such a vanquished air was about him that if the corpse left behind didn't prove otherwise, anyone who saw him couldn't have guessed he had won.

His weary steps eventually led him to the top of the mountain, where a lonely stone tower stood perched on a naturally formed ledge. It was virtually indistinguishable from the living rock around it.

There was something quite peculiar about that tower, Athanor observed. It had neither windows nor doors, no visible point of entry. Where its doorway would have normally been, spread a slimy membrane, full of red veins and faintly pulsing with a life of its own.

Athanor approached, dragging his sword behind him. He was half-expecting a new horror to tear through the membrane and attack him at any moment.

He was prepared to let the monster win that time. It could do what it wished with his preternatural flesh. Perhaps, that way, he could finally find some measure of rest.

He brought his fingertips up to the membrane, feeling its leathery slime-flecked surface. It was warm to the touch, unlike everything else in Irkala Kar.

Through it, he could see the shadowy outlines of people coming and going, some crouching down on their knees and raising their hands to the sky as if to offer a prayer.

He had to stare long and hard at that soundless play of blurred shadows for some time before realizing what he was looking at.

It was the world above, he realized, seen from the inside of a grave at some cemetery, where the living came to bring funeral offerings to the tombs of their loved ones.

Athanor began pounding against the membrane with both hands frantically, trying to break through. A faint whisper for help surfaced from his parched throat, barely audible. When that didn't work, he fell upon it with his entire body again and again. In vain.

A fervent desire to return to the life he once knew seized him and he fought even harder to break the barrier separating the two worlds.

As if to tease him cruelly, the membrane proved to be very elastic, allowing him to hope that he could penetrate it with enough effort but, in the end, it refused to break.

Even when Athanor tried to force it with the edge of his sword, frothing at the mouth and spitting incoherent curses, it would not give in. It remained impregnable and all of his whimpering and crying failed to reach the shades of the living on the other side.

After what seemed endless attempts to break through, Athanor finally gave up and sank to his knees before the tower's leathery entrance.

"There's no escape from Irkala Kar", a voice said. It came distinct and clear, only a few feet away from him. "At least that's what the gods say".

Athanor turned abruptly. He was certain that he would see no one there and finally prove to himself that insanity had completely overcome him.

Much to his surprise, he saw the figure of a tall slender man. His head was large, too large, oblong even, and his limps where like stretched out ribbons, fluttering in the wind.

His attire or characteristics were not clearly visible, as if shadowed perpetually by a dim light that only allowed glimpses of a somewhat human form with piercing eyes and a red mouth full of fish-like fangs.

"But what do the gods know, right?" the shadowy figure went on, gliding closer to Athanor.

"Who are you?" Athanor retorted, quickly jumping to his feet and raising his sword.

The shadowy figure scoffed.

"I've had so many names throughout the eons that I've really lost count", it said. "But that's not important right now. I've come to talk to you about your impending judgement".

"This again", Athanor snarled and lashed out

at the thing.

His blade swooshed harmlessly through the slender ethereal form and the figure of penumbral light laughed an icy laugh.

"Feisty. I like that! That's why I chose you", it said.

"You... you chose me?"

"Sit down, my body. Sit down. It's time you learned some things about this place".

There was something unsettling in the way that thing pronounced 'my body' – as if it wanted to say 'my boy', but its grasp on human language was lacking.

"The only thing I care to learn about this hell is how to escape from it", Athanor cried, making another ineffective attempt to attack the thing of shadow and half-light.

"All in good time, all in good time, my body. I swear that you, the recently deceased, are such children sometimes".

IX

LAPIS ANIMAE

The penumbral man's voice was deep and had a soothing effect, like the whispers of a wetnurse. There was something ominously sarcastic about his tone and sometimes his phrasing became unapologetically irrational, as if to tease sanity. His words were coils of smoke, enveloping Athanor's attention and captivating it.

He told him how all paths in the Underworld inevitably led to the Hall of Judgement, where the old gods dwelt.

There, they welcomed the purified dead, after they had received purgation at the hands of the guardians at the gates. Their tortured bodies were burnt to a crisp until nothing remained but a sole gem, the *lapis animae*.

The soul stone was then picked up and taken to a single ray of sunlight, punching through from the world above. It was placed there for the same purposed that gold is put to the dissolving test of purity: gf the gem was transparent and caused a rainbow spectrum to appear, then the soul of the deceased was given a new body and ensured safe passage on the Dawn Courser.

The Dawn Courser was the ship that ferried the souls of the vindicated dead on a daily journey to the world above. They were allowed the entirety of the day to enjoy the sunlight and all the pleasant memories of their former lives. At night, they returned to Irkala Kar and slept the sleep of oblivion in mausoleums prepared for them on some sundered shore, until their next voyage.

The evil dead, however, were given a

deformed body and sent back to wander again through the horrors of the Underworld and to be slaughtered endless times by the guardians at the gates, in an infinite loop of soul-flaying agony.

"So, you're telling me I've been going about this all wrong?" Athanor asked caustically. "That I broke the rules?"

"I do not concern myself with right and wrong. I was here long before the gods were banished to this place and presumed to become judge, jury, and executioner. I was born when Irkala Kar was born and she is me as much as I am part of her".

"So, what do you want from me?"

"The question is what do *you* want? Do you want this to be your lot, my body? Granted, you are not like the rest of the sheep; but even a king in hell is a creature more miserable than the meanest of mortals".

"I want to see the sun again. I want to feel the breeze of the sea on my face once more. I want to remember my daughters' faces, the kisses of my wife". Athanor mumbled.

"Excellent", the slender figure's limbs quivered with a strange excitment. "And what are you prepared to do for this?"

"Anything; everything!" Athanor blurted out. "But you said before, there is no escape from this place".

"That is true. You can't escape from Irkala Kar any more than I can… if, however, the two were to become one, then you would no longer be you and I would no longer be me".

"I do not understand".

"Long have I been on the lookout for someone like you, my body. A human host for my being – one driven enough by the fire of anger, an unrepentant heart that reviles judgement. If our essences were to merge, then we would be an entirely new being. Half you, my blood-crazed body, and half I, eternal egregor of the Underworld. And a being like that… well, it could stand a chance of escaping this never-ending nightmare, onboard the Dawn Courser".

"But you said only the vindicated dead get to be onboard that ship".

"Yes, when the gods are watching. But say someone were to distract their attention long enough for a stowaway to creep onboard; someone of immense power, capable of standing up to them long enough to cause them a headache… then things would be different, would they not?"

"And you would do this for me? Why?"

"I would do this for us. If you agree to a merging of essences, there will no longer be 'I' and 'you'. There will only be 'we'. We will be just like the place where day and night meet on the earth. We would be twilight and we would be the break of dawn".

Athanor shook his head.

"And how do I know you'll keep your end of the bargain?"

"I have nothing to gain from harming you, my body. Besides, what are you afraid I might do to you? Kill you?" the specter laughed frightfully. "I need you on that boat – just as you need me to thwart the judgement of the gods".

Athanor remained silent for a long moment.

The words of the penumbral man resonated in some dark corner of his heart. They slaked the thirst of his parched soul and eased the icy clutch of fear stifling his very being.

Judgement divine would surely find him deserving of eternal damnation, he thought. After all, had he not wished ill on those he pretended to love? Had he not abandoned them to slaughter, like a coward? It would be madness to deliver himself into the hands of angry gods.

Though he knew he deserved to be punished, he refused to accept it in death from the very gods that had abandoned him in life. A powerful and proud vein in his soul rebelled at the idea of being reduced to a *lapis animae*, a piece of crystal for the gods to play with.

"Alright", he said at last with a heavy sigh.

"Let's do this".

The penumbral man pulled back his red mouth in a leer, visible only for a split second.

"Splendid. Go forth, then. Embrace your judgment", even as he spoke he began to vanish, like dispersing mist.

"Wait! Aren't you coming with me?"

"Just call my name and I'll be there".

"What *is* your name?" Athanor pleaded desperately, for the penumbral man was all but disappeared.

"Sarkany", a faint whisper echoed all around him.

Athanor found himself all alone once more, with his back resting on the tower's membranous entrance.

Behind him, the distorted shadowy forms of

mortals paying their last respects before the graves of their own played like a grotesque theatre of unholy thoughts being projected from his mind.

X

ESCAPE FROM IRKALA KAR

Athanor descended from the mountainside in leaps and bounds that defied gravity, with his grisly scarab wings buzzing.

Great flatlands of ashen grey spread out before him. At the westernmost edge of the askew horizon, an unmoving ocean stretched shimmering and glass-like. Where the ocean's surf lapped the barren shoreline, rose the Hall of Judgement.

The palace of the old gods was a magnificent structure of porphyry, built in the ancient architectural style of the opulent temples of the Pangeans. Its pillars were of chalcedony and radiant jewels encrusted their massive capitals.

A roofed archway, completely covered with long-dead ivy leaves, led to its entrance. It formed a causeway, stretching into the flatlands for what seemed like an entire mile.

Athanor landed before it with a heavy thud and, as his feet disturbed the untrodden threshold, a thick cloud of ashes and dust rose to envelop him.

He felt heavy as he entered the archway, as if weighted down by an unseen burden. Every step seemed to require excruciating effort and the sinking in heart grew exponentially at the thought of what awaited him ahead.

Colossal pillars of marble rose on either side of him and made him feel like a dwarf, an insignificant little creature intruding in the abode of his betters.

His footsteps echoed in empty archway and, without even realizing it, he caught himself counting them as if they were his last.

It took forever to reach the Hall of Judgment proper – and that forever passed in the blink of an eye. There were no doors to the Hall. The way was open, leading from the archway to a cyclopean rotunda of porphyry.

Although no lamp or torch could be seen, a sickly crimson phosphorescence radiated from the very pores of the walls. The interior of the rotunda was constructed in three concentric rings, spanning on different levels and interconnected by a vertical staircase of lapis lazuli which led to the innermost ring.

There, at its center, stood a basaltic pedestal of great proportions. All around it, rose towering and brooding the statues of the twelve old gods.

Athanor began ascending the steps leading to the pedestal. His knees were shaky and his footing unsure.

Suddenly, a commanding voice boomed, seemingly coming from every direction at once. It was not a human voice at all. It was more of a sound, horribly metallic and cacophonous, as if a throng of voices – male and female alike – screeched in perfected unison. Their tones were eerily harmonized, creating a terrible and awe-inspiring music. The words they spoke where in no language Athanor knew and yet he could understand them perfectly in some irrational part of his mind.

"Step forth and lay bare thy deeds".

There was something quintessentially commanding and powerful in the way these words were voiced that Athanor didn't even think for an instant not to obey.

He climbed onto the pedestal and looked at

the unblinking, stern faces of the gods surrounding him.

"Are you ready to receive the cleansing flame and let thy truth be made manifest?" the cacophonous divine harmony asked.

Athanor's limbs were loosened. His sword clattered on the floor. He closed his beryl eyes and swallowed hard.

"Sarkany", he cried out in his mind, "Deliver me, Sarkany. Come to me now; come!"

Great tongues of flame leapt up from the base of the pedestal but abruptly they died down, before even singeing him.

A deep subterranean rumbling echoed throughout the rotunda and the Hall of Judgement shook violently as if seized in the throes of an earthquake.

The ebon rafters of its roof cracked, and its foundations began to quiver. A rain of small detritus started coming down from the domed ceiling, crashing around Athanor like hail.

A mournful cry arose from the statues of the gods. It was a beautiful and poignant sound, suffused with unspeakable melancholy and a fear that no creature under the sun could ever express or imagine.

One by one, the statues began shaking and rocking on their bases until they toppled one upon the other like dominos, finally collapsing onto the floor and shattering to a million pieces.

Out of the debris of each statue, a pathetic mummified creature emerged, dazed and feeble and bewildered. Some were partially covered in blood-cackled bandages while others were completely naked, revealing a malformed mixture of animal and human limbs.

Those with more life left in them began running all around, like startled sleep, while others merely crawled, trying to get back into the dark hollows of their broken effigies.

Thunder pealed resoundingly and the dome of the Hall of Judgment, together with its floor, were rent asunder. The porphyry walls began bleeding and squirming, as if they had been transformed into lumps of tortured flesh.

Athanor knew that this was his moment. He picked up his sword instinctively and lounged down the stairs, leaping high in the air and beating his scarab wings with all the might he could muster, to gain more ground.

Behind him, he could hear the poignantly melodious screeching of the gods as their temple was collapsing in on itself. Above the rumble and the crashing of ruin echoed the piercing, cold laughter of Sarkany, like a gust of wind shuffling through the marbled halls.

Athanor fled, spurred on by a sense of dread and haste such as he had never before known. He switched spasmodically between running, crawling on all fours and leaping into the air like a hunted animal. It wasn't his life that was at stake. It was his very being.

Every distorted muscle in his unnatural body was committed to the task and his heart was pounding like a frenzied drum, endowing him with an agility he had never imagined he could possess.

Like a curse out of the mouth of hell, he came speeding out in the open. Only a split second later, the threshold of the Hall of Judgment came crashing down in a heap of rubble behind him.

He did not pause in his maddened flight, though. In the distance, he could see the clear shimmering of black waters; and standing out against the blackness, was the shape of a boat – the Dawn Courser – patiently waiting to be manned by its crew of the vindicated ones.

Athanor's mind was no longer processing thoughts. It was fixed on a single purpose.

He struck the still waters like a cannon ball of flesh and waded through them in a frenzy, finally managing to grab hold of the ship's railing and pull himself onboard.

For a few moments, he just lay there breathing hard, in short, tortured rasps. The exhilarating realization that he had made it was quickly settling in. But what was to follow? His eye fell upon a large chest of pure ivory, near the prow.

It was large enough to hold a man of his size. He couldn't have asked for a more ideal hiding place.

Crawling on all fours, for no other reason than to appease a paranoid impulse of avoiding detection by the vindicated dead soon to arrive, he climbed into the chest and shut the lid over his head. It felt like voluntarily shutting himself in his own coffin – and the sensation brought him a morbid sort of relief.

Cramped and alone in the confined darkness, he waited. Perhaps, he thought, the Dawn Courser would never set sail, and this was all some sick joke played upon him by the penumbral man. Or, perhaps, it was a matter of time before he was found out. Perhaps his sins reeked of anathema, and he had merely succeeded in making himself an easy target for the guardians of the ship.

Such thoughts rapidly spiraling towards schizophrenia were cut abruptly when he heard distant singing approaching.

Before long, footsteps creaked on the deck of the ship and he could hear gentle voices talking amongst themselves of things of the world above: mundane things, the little joys of everyday life.

The sound alone was so alien to his ears. And the images such words invoked filled his beryl eyes with tears and a fierce bitterness for all that he had been denied.

The ship began to move. Water slushed on the sides of its hull as it slid across the water and gradually gained speed, even though there was no wind to impel it onwards. The speed kept increasing and increasing, reaching a gut-wrenching momentum, until he could feel they were cutting through the air like an arrow.

A hope beyond all hope flickered in his heart. He had made it. He was free. He was leaving the Underworld and he would finally get his second chance amongst the living.

His breath was suddenly caught short. The darkness inside the chest seemed to come alive. His fingers clenched until his knuckles turned white. A violent seizure of nausea raked his whole body and pain exploded in his every nerve ending.

"I am here", a familiar voice whispered inside his mind.

"Sarkany".

"Call me Freedom", the voice chuckled.

The Dawn Courser was rapidly climbing to the heavens above, parting the ashen clouds in its wake. It was head straight for a narrow opening in the membranous dome that yawned like an infected larynx. Its walls were contracting with eerie life and oozing a blood-red dew.

At the end of the tunnel, immeasurably far and yet within reach, a brilliant light shone with the promise of the world above.

The vindicated ones on the deck were singing a joyous hymn, praising this ever-approaching light. A grateful bliss flooded their minds at the prospect of once more tasting the splendors of an ordinary day under the sun.

It was then that the chest was kicked open from the inside and Athanor emerged. At least, what used to be Athanor.

The man standing now before the vindicated dead, with his saw-edged sword in both hands, was as pale as a relentless winter morning. His leering mouth was redder than the opened insides of a sacrifice and his beryl eyes were enveloped in a black shadow, as if smoke had been trapped within the precious stones.

The joyous hymn fell silent and the glad faces were poisoned by dismay and dread. The eyes of the innocent were helplessly fixed at this nightmarish thing that had somehow found its way into their protected abode of bliss.

The creature that once was Athanor turned its darkened, inhuman eyes to the boatswain. A glimmer of envy flashed across them.

The man steering the boat towards the light looked exactly like Athanor once did, in happier days and years gone by.

A loud roar of avenging fury erupted from the

fiend's lips as it lounged forward, swinging its blood-stained blade. The massacre that followed was swift, yet excruciatingly thorough.

The immaculate deck of the Dawn Courser was left swimming in gore. Voices that only moments before sang full of hope for the sun, were now gurgling death throes and pitiful screams. Mangled corpses fell overboard and disappeared into the void below in a rain of tattered flesh.

The Athanor fiend spared no one; but he saved the one who looked like his former self for last.

"Coward", he cursed in maddened fury as he swung his blade to open the gut of his eerie doppelganger. "You left her alone. You left her all alone when she needed you! It should have been you; you, you cowardly bastard! Now give me the sun!"

He kept hacking at the man, turning his body

into a crimson pulp. Each time he pulled back his sword, bits of flesh and bone were torn off by the cruel edges of his weapon. With every blow he dealt the words coming out of his mouth grew less and less coherent, until they finally turned to the mere snarls of a demon.

When there was nothing else left to hack at, he tossed the mangled remains of his victim overboard.

He tried to let go of his sword but saw that he couldn't. His fingers had been fused around the hilt. It was now part of him.

The light at the end of the tunnel was almost upon him. He closed his weary eyes and smiled, licking the blood from his red lips.

The next time he opened them he wanted to see the world he knew as a mortal. That bitter and beautiful world, where the sun shone on green pastures and blue oceans.

He could feel rebirth was at hand. It was flowing like fire in his veins. And this time around, he would do everything right. Without apologizing, without regrets, without hesitation. With the sword.

The light grew ever brighter, until all was a searing whiteness. Shattered time was restored, and dimensions fell back into order.

All Athanor could hear was the pounding of his own heart and the reverberation of his shallow breathing. What a beautiful symphony of life these two made!

Yet, something else was there as well. Another pulse, a breath whose rhythm was alien to his own. The difference was subtle but its presence undeniable.

For every thought he had, another sprung to answer it in cold, mocking tones. For everything noble and good his heart desired, he also made a wish for monstrous things. Impulses arose in him that were not *of* him. His very perception of reality felt as if it had been split in two.

At that moment he knew he would never be alone again.

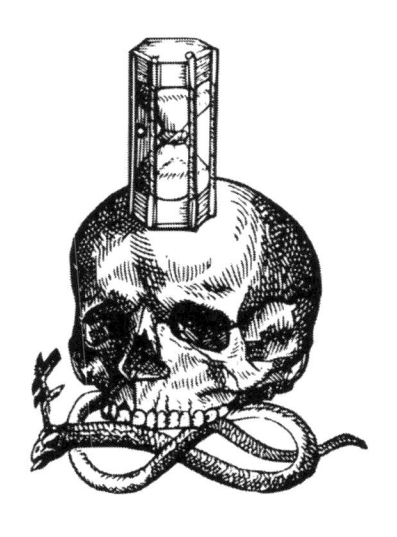

ABOUT THE AUTHOR

Marios Koutsoukos was born in August, 1983. He is a bilingual author, writing in both his native Greek and in English.

He has a degree of French Language and Literature, a Masters in Creative Writing, and is currently a PhD candidate in Classics.

Since 2004, he has been collaborating as a lyricist with metal bands and artists from around the world.

For more information, news, books and random blog artciles, feel free to visit his website:

www.marioskoutsoukos.com

Printed in Great Britain
by Amazon